To my wife

Balzer + Bray is an imprint of HarperCollins Publishers.

Knuffle Bunny Free: An Unexpected Diversion
Copyright © 2010 by Mo Willems
All rights reserved. Manufactured in China.

Library of Congress Cataloging-in-Publication Data is
available.
ISBN 978-0-06-192957-1 (trade bdg.)
ISBN 978-0-06-192958-8 (lib. bdg.)

The illustrations in this book are rendered by hand in ink,
then colored and composited in digital collage.
Typography by Martha Rago
17 18 SCP 10 9 8
❖ First Edition

KNUFFLE BUNNY FREE

AN UNEXPECTED DIVERSION BY Mo Willems

BALZER + BRAY / AN IMPRINT OF HARPERCOLLINSPUBLISHERS

One day, not so long ago,
Trixie took a big trip with her family.

They were on their way to visit
Trixie's "Oma" and "Opa" in Holland.

Holland is far away.

So that meant taking
a taxi to the airport,

waiting in line,

watching Knuffle Bunny
go through the big machine,

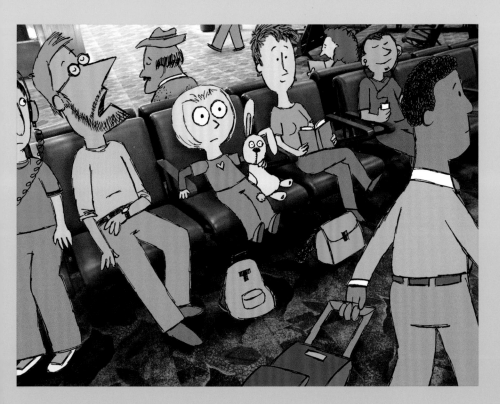

waiting some more,

and (finally) getting onto a real airplane!

On the plane,
Trixie played

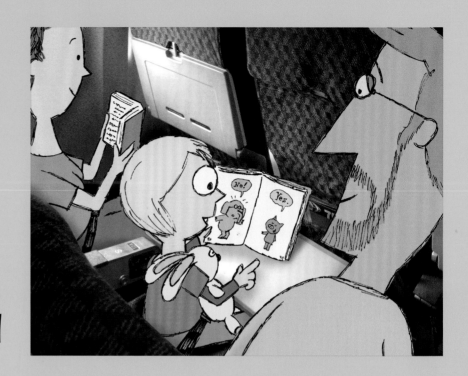

and read

and slept.

Before she knew it,
the plane had landed.

Trixie and her family left the
airport and got on a train
to go to . . .

Oma and Opa's house!

Oma and Opa were so happy to see Trixie!

Soon Oma and Trixie were drinking cold glasses of chocolate milk in the garden.

Suddenly Trixie realized something!

Trixie didn't tell
her daddy that
Knuffle Bunny
was gone.

She didn't have to.

Trixie's daddy called the airline and asked them to look for Knuffle Bunny on the plane.

But the plane had left for **China.**

China is **very** far away. . . .

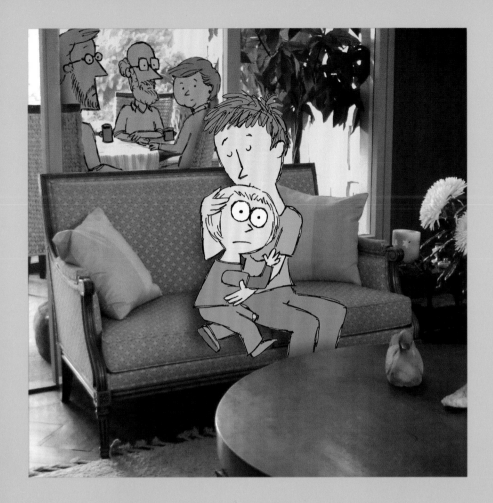

Trixie's mommy hugged her
and asked her to be brave.

Trixie's daddy told the story
of when he was a little boy
and said good-bye to his
"Special Lamby."

Oma gave Trixie another glass of chocolate milk and remarked on how big she was getting.

Trixie understood.

She was getting bigger.

The next morning, Trixie tried to enjoy going to the café

and the
swings in the
playground

and the carnival
that was in town.

And while the whole week was filled with fun things, like eating French fries on the street,

visiting real windmills,
and feeding the ducks,

Trixie was still sad.

She missed her Knuffle Bunny.

(Oma and Opa understood.)

(Oma and Opa had a plan.)

That night, they had a surprise for Trixie: a brand-new, top-of-the-line

FUNNY-BUNNY-WUNNY-DOLL™ EXTREME!

It could walk!

It could speak!
(In Dutch.)

t could dance!

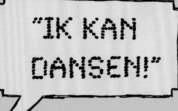

But it couldn't make Trixie feel any better.

She dreamed of all the children

and all the places he would visit.

She dreamed of Knuffle Bunny

Trixie was sure that she wouldn't be able
to sleep another night in a strange bed
without her Knuffle Bunny.

But before she knew it,

she was dreaming. . . .

Trixie had a big breakfast.

She played with Oma on the playground swings.

Knuffle Bunny would meet.

She dreamed of how Knuffle Bunny would make them feel better.

The next morning,
Trixie felt better.

She even tried a sip of Opa's coffee at the café!

It was a great day.

Before she knew it, the trip was over and it was time to go home.
Trixie hugged Oma and Opa as hard as she could.

Then Trixie and her family got back onto the train,

and back onto the plane,

and listened to the crying baby as the plane lifted off.

But can you believe it?
Right there, on that very plane,

Trixie noticed something. . . .

Trixie was so happy to have Knuffle Bunny back in her arms.

Happy enough to make
a decision. . . .

Trixie turned around
and said:

Would your
baby like my
Knuffle Bunny?

"Really?"

asked the baby's mother.

"Really?"

asked Trixie's daddy.

"Really?"

asked Trixie's mommy.

"BlAggie PlAggie?"

asked the baby.

said Trixie. She was big enough.

The baby was happy.
The baby's mother was thankful.
Trixie's parents were proud.

And the other passengers
were very relieved.

And that is how,

a few weeks later,

Trixie received her very first letter!

The end.

A NOTE TO TRIXIE:

TRIXIE, I HOPE TO WATCH YOU GROW UP,

FALL IN LOVE,

START A FAMILY, AND BE HAPPY.

AND I HOPE THAT ONE DAY,
MANY YEARS FROM NOW,

YOU WILL RECEIVE A PACKAGE

. . . FROM AN OLD PEN PAL.

LOVE,
DADDY

Special thanks to:

Rob Gussenhoven, American Airlines, the Port Authority of
NY & NJ, the TSA, Ambassador Scieszka, the Lewine family,
Giorgio Balzer, the real Oma, Opa, Mommy, and especially Trixie.